To
Joseph and Luke,
and Faith and Damien.

THIS IS A BORZOI BOOK PUBLISHED BY ALFRED A. KNOPF

Copyright © 2003 by David Lucas
All rights reserved under International and Pan-American Copyright Conventions.
Published in the United States of America by Alfred A. Knopf, an imprint of Random House
Children's Books, a division of Random House, Inc., New York. Distributed by Random
House, Inc., New York. Originally published in Great Britain in 2003 by Andersen Press Ltd.,
20 Vauxhall Bridge Road, London SW1V 2SA.
www.randomhouse.com/kids
KNOPF, BORZOI BOOKS, and the colophon are registered trademarks of Random House, Inc.

Library of Congress Cataloging-in-Publication Data available upon request

ISBN 0-375-82690-4 (trade) • ISBN 0-375-92690-9 (lib. bdg.)

PRINTED IN ITALY • February 2004

10 9 8 7 6 5 4 3 2

First American Edition

Halibut Jackson

by David Lucas

Alfred A. Knopf
New York

Halibut Jackson was *shy*.

Halibut Jackson didn't like to be noticed.

Halibut Jackson liked to blend into the *background*.

He had a suit that he wore to the *park*.

He had a suit that he wore to the *shops*.

He had a suit that he wore to the *library*.

But mostly Halibut Jackson stayed *indoors*.

One day a letter arrived. It was an INVITATION.
An invitation on a scroll of silver and gold.
It was an invitation to a *party*.

Her Majesty the Queen
would like to invite you to her
Grand Birthday Party.

Please come to the Palace
next Saturday.

RSVP

"The Palace!" said Halibut Jackson.
He had seen *pictures* of the Palace.
How he longed to see the Palace for himself.
The Palace was *silver* and *gold* and covered in *jewels*.

But Halibut Jackson was *shy*.
Halibut Jackson didn't like to be noticed.
Halibut Jackson *certainly* didn't go to parties.
What a shame!

That night, he dreamed of the Palace.
He dreamed of *glittering* towers, of *silver* stairs,
of a *golden* door . . .

And when he woke, he had an *idea*.

He began to make a SUIT,
a suit of *silver* and *gold,* covered with *jewels.*

"Now nobody will even notice me,"
said Halibut Jackson.

How was he to know it was a *garden party*?

Everybody noticed Halibut Jackson.

And *everybody* wanted a suit like his.
"What a BEAUTIFUL suit!" they said.

"Can you make *me* a suit of SILVER?" said the Queen.
"Can you make *me* a suit of GOLD?" said the King.

"I will do my best . . . ," said Halibut Jackson.

And so Halibut Jackson made a suit for the Queen,
and a suit for the King.
Halibut Jackson made suits for *everybody*.

Before long, Halibut Jackson had opened a *shop*,
a shop selling all kinds of clothes,
every kind of suit and hat that he could think of.
In big *gold* letters, a sign said: HALIBUT JACKSON.

Now Halibut Jackson had friends.
Now Halibut Jackson had plenty to do.

And although he was still a little *shy*,
it seemed not to matter so very much at all.